DRAGON MASTERS

FUTURE OF THE TIME DRAGON

BY

TRACEY WEST

SCHOLASTIC INC.

DRAGON MASTERS
Read All the Adventures

Special Edition!

More books coming soon!

TABLE OF CONTENTS

TO THE MEMBERS OF FRANCESCA'S BOOK CLUB.

Our friendship will stand the test of time. — TW

Text copyright © 2020 by Tracey West
Illustrations copyright © 2020 by Scholastic Inc.

All rights reserved. Published by Scholastic Inc., *Publishers since 1920.* SCHOLASTIC, BRANCHES, and associated logos are trademarks and/or registered trademarks of Scholastic Inc. The publisher does not have any control over and does not assume any responsibility for author or third-party websites or their content.

No part of this publication may be reproduced, stored in a retrieval system, or transmitted in any form or by any means, electronic, mechanical, photocopying, recording, or otherwise, without written permission of the publisher. For information regarding permission, write to Scholastic Inc., Attention: Permissions Department, 557 Broadway, New York, NY 10012.

This book is a work of fiction. Names, characters, places, and incidents are either the product of the author's imagination or are used fictitiously, and any resemblance to actual persons, living or dead, business establishments, events, or locales is entirely coincidental.

Library of Congress Cataloging-in-Publication Data
Names: West, Tracey, 1965- author. | Griffo, Daniel, illustrator. | West, Tracey, 1965- Dragon Masters; 15.
Title: Future of the Time Dragon / by Tracey West; illustrated by Daniel Griffo.
Description: First edition. | New York, NY : Branches/Scholastic Inc., 2020.
| Series: Dragon masters; 15 | Summary: The dark wizard Maldred has trapped Dragon Master Eko as well as wizards who have opposed him, all of them frozen in time and space inside a wall in his hideout; so Drake and Worm set out to seek the help of the Time Dragon—but when an imp named Beezel interferes Drake ends up back in his own past, and he must find a way to get back to the present.
Identifiers: LCCN 2018058500 | ISBN 9781338540253 (pbk.) | ISBN 9781338540260 (hardcover)
Subjects: LCSH: Dragons—Juvenile fiction. | Magic—Juvenile fiction. | Wizards—Juvenile fiction. Time travel—Juvenile fiction. Adventure stories. CYAC: Dragons—Fiction. Magic—Fiction. | Wizards—Fiction. Time travel—Fiction. Adventure and adventurers—Fiction. | LCGFT: Action and adventure fiction.
Classification: LCC PZ7.W51937 Fw 2020 | DDC 813.54 [Fic]—dc23 LC record available at https://lccn.loc.gov/2018058500

10 9 8 7 6 5 4 3   20 21 22 23 24

Printed in the U.S.A.   23

First edition, March 2020
Illustrated by Daniel Griffo
Edited by Katie Carella
Book design by Sarah Dvojack

A RESCUE MISSION

Eat up, Worm," Drake said. "We need to be strong for our next mission."

Drake handed another apple to his big brown Earth Dragon. Worm gobbled it down.

Drake and Worm were in the Dragon Caves in King Roland's castle. Drake had gotten a good night's sleep. His belly was full of eggs and potatoes. He had eaten breakfast earlier with the other Dragon Masters — Rori, Bo, Ana, and Petra.

"We almost never got to rest when we were trying to stop Maldred," Drake told Worm. "We traveled all over the world. And we barely ate or slept. But we're ready for our next adventure."

Drake and the Dragon Masters had stopped Maldred, the evil wizard, from destroying the world with an Earthquake Dragon called the Naga. But Drake's kingdom, Bracken, had been damaged by an earthquake. So Drake and Worm had traveled to find the Spring Dragon. She had brought the land back to life.

But one more person still needed their help.

"Drake, it's time to leave! We have to find Eko," Rori said, running into the caves. "Are you ready yet?"

Eko was a Dragon Master, too. The last time they saw her, Maldred made her disappear. Last night, Eko's Thunder Dragon, Neru, had asked the Dragon Masters to find her. Drake and Rori had volunteered for the mission.

"Almost," Drake replied. He walked over to Neru and gave him an apple. The purple dragon gulped it down. "That should do it. Ready, Worm?"

The bright green Dragon Stone Drake wore around his neck glowed. It meant he was connecting with his dragon. Every Dragon Master wore a piece of the Dragon Stone.

He heard Worm's voice inside his head. *Ready.*

"Finally!" Rori said. She led her Fire Dragon, Vulcan, out of his cave. "Let's go!"

THE WIZARD'S HIDEOUT

Drake, Worm, Rori, Vulcan, and Neru all made their way over to the Training Room. Griffith the wizard was waiting for them there. So were Ana, Bo, and Petra.

"Eko went missing from inside Maldred's hideout, so we should begin our search there," Griffith said. "Drake, can Worm get us there?"

I can do it, Worm told Drake. *The hideout is located in a magical space, but I can connect to the energy you left behind when you were there.*

Drake nodded to Griffith. "He can."

"You three must watch over the castle while we are gone," Griffith told Ana, Bo, and Petra.

"We will," said Bo.

"Good luck!" Petra added.

Ana ran over and hugged Rori.

Drake touched Worm. Rori touched Vulcan and Worm. Griffith touched Neru and Vulcan. Now that they were all connected to Worm, they could transport.

"To Maldred's hideout!" Drake cried.

Green light exploded. Drake's stomach flip-flopped. When the light faded, Drake blinked. They were in a room filled with potions and books: Maldred's workshop.

"We made it!" Drake cried, patting Worm.

"Eko, are you here?" Rori called out.

Her voice echoed through the tall, round tower. A spiral staircase led from the bottom floor all the way to the top.

"We should search one floor at a time," Griffith said.

Drake shivered. "Even though Maldred's not here, this is still a spooky place."

Rori nodded. "I'm glad we trapped him in that bottle."

"And I'm *really* glad the bottle is hidden deep inside the earth," Drake added.

"I hope Maldred never gets out!" Rori said.

Suddenly, Drake had an eerie feeling that somebody was watching them.

"Yes," Drake agreed. "Let's hope he stays trapped forever."

Then Drake heard Worm's voice inside his head. *Neru can sense Eko. He says she is at the top of the tower.*

"Eko is upstairs!" Drake cried.

THE WEIRD WALL

They all hurried to the top of the tower. Drake gazed around. The light was dim, but he could see a design of painted faces on the curved wall. Drake remembered this strange wall from when he and Rori had first come to the hideout.

"Eko, where are you?" Rori called out.

Neru can't see Eko, but he feels her, Worm told Drake.

"Neru said he can feel Eko," Drake said. "He can't see her, but he's sure she's here. Did Maldred make her invisible?"

Griffith, meanwhile, had moved closer to the wall. He stared at it.

"This is very interesting," he said. "I know some of these faces. They are wizards!"

Drake gave the faces on the wall a closer look. There were men and women. Some of them wore pointy hats. Some of the men had long beards, like Griffith's.

"None of these faces look happy," Rori remarked. "They all look scared or angry."

"Did Maldred paint this wall?" Drake asked.

"I fear it is much worse," Griffith replied. He pointed to a face on the wall, a man with a long mustache. "This is Berg of the Misty Mountains. He went missing twenty years ago. We always suspected that Maldred had something to do with it."

Rori frowned, thinking. "He went missing. And now his face is on Maldred's wall..."

Griffith nodded. "Maldred must have used dark magic to trap these wizards inside the wall."

Rori turned pale. "If he trapped people inside this wall, then maybe . . ."

She ran around the circular hallway, looking at the wall. Drake followed her. She stopped quickly, and Drake skidded to a stop behind her.

Rori pointed at the wall with a shaking hand.

Staring at them from the wall was the face of a young woman. Her mouth was open in shock.

"It's Eko!" Rori yelled.

CHAPTER 4

STRONG MAGIC

Drake stared at Eko's face on the wall. Goose bumps popped up on his arms.

She is trapped in the wall, he realized, *looking out at us.*

Griffith and the dragons crowded around.

"Poor Eko," Griffith said. "She made a bad choice when she decided to help Maldred. But she did not deserve this."

"Maldred did this to her because she was trying to help us," Rori reminded him. Tears glistened in her eyes. "Hurry, Griffith! Use your magic. You've got to get her out of there!"

Griffith frowned. "It's not that simple," he said. "Eko and these wizards are not just trapped in the wall. I believe they are trapped in *time* as well. Berg does not look any older than he did when he first went missing."

"Can you cast a spell to free them?" Rori asked.

The wizard shook his head. "Maldred used very powerful magic to do this."

Drake thought about when they had been in trouble before. Many times, a dragon had solved the problem. "Is there a dragon that could help us?"

The wizard stroked his beard. "That is an excellent thought, Drake. There is a Time Dragon in the Land of Casgore. He may be our only hope."

"Then let's go to Casgore!" Rori cried.

"I will stay here and search Maldred's workshop for the spell he used to trap Eko and the others. If I can find it, maybe I can undo it," Griffith said.

Neru wants to stay here, too, Worm told Drake. *He wants to watch over Eko.*

Drake glanced at the Thunder Dragon. Neru was staring sadly at the wall.

"Neru is going to stay here," Drake told the others.

"Fine," said Rori. "But can we please hurry and get to Casgore?"

"Of course," Drake replied. "But Casgore is a big place. How will we find the Time Dragon?"

"Come with me. There should be maps in Maldred's library," Griffith said.

They returned to Maldred's workshop at the base of the tower. Griffith quickly found a map of Casgore.

"The Time Dragon lives on top of this mountain," Griffith said, pointing.

Drake leaned over to look at the map. "Worm, can you get us there?" he asked.

Yes, Worm replied.

"We're ready," Drake told Rori. As he touched Worm with one hand, he felt an itch on his neck. He tried to scratch it, but the itch was already gone.

Rori placed one hand on Worm and one hand on Vulcan.

"Worm, please transport us to the Time Dragon!" Drake commanded.

THE DRAGON
IN THE MOUNTAINS

They transported to Casgore in a flash of green light. Drake immediately started shivering. He looked around.

They were surrounded by huge snowy mountaintops and a bright blue sky. In front of them stood a white house with a red peaked roof. Behind it rose a tall tower made of stone as blue as the sky. The tower looked out over a forest of green trees and a shimmering blue lake.

"It's beautiful here," Drake said.

"And cold," Rori added. "Now let's find that dragon."

As she spoke, a blond-haired boy stepped out of the house. He wore a black vest over his white shirt. His black pants were tucked into brown boots. And a green Dragon Stone glittered around his neck.

"What are you doing here?" the boy asked them.

"We're Dragon Masters, just like you," Drake replied. "We're here because we need your help."

"We need the Time Dragon to break a spell that trapped people in time," Rori added.

The boy grinned. "Looks like you're in the right place at the right *time*," he said. His Dragon Stone glowed and he closed his eyes. A few seconds later, he opened them.

"Maj, the Time Dragon, says he will see you," the boy said. "And I am Lukas, his Dragon Master."

Drake and Rori introduced themselves.

"Now I will take you to meet Maj," Lukas said.

They followed Lukas to the stone tower. "I have a question for you. Why did the man throw the clock out the window?" he asked as they walked.

"That's a strange question," Rori said.

Lukas smiled. "He wanted to see time fly. Get it? It's a riddle."

Rori groaned, but Drake smiled. *Lukas seems friendly*, he thought.

Lukas opened the tower door and they stepped inside, followed by the two dragons. A very tall clock stood in the center of the room. It was not like any clock Drake had ever seen. It had three clock faces with many gears spinning behind them. The first face was a big circle with lines around it and two spinning hands. Above the first face, the second had numbers and three hands. The third, smallest face was above the second face. It had just one hand that was shaped like an arrow. Strange symbols were painted around the face.

Perched above the clock was a dark blue dragon with red spikes. He had leathery wings, four legs, and a snout curved like a bird's beak.

"Maj, this is Drake and Rori. They are Dragon Masters," Lukas said.

The Time Dragon's body glowed with blue light. Then streams of light flowed from his eyes and zapped Drake and Rori.

Drake's whole body felt tingly. "What's happening?" he cried.

ANY TIME, ANY PLACE

The bright blue light kept streaming from the Time Dragon's eyes.

"Tell your dragon to stop!" Rori yelled.

"Maj is just taking a look at your past," Lukas said. "To see if you have caused harm to others."

The blue light faded, and Drake's body stopped tingling.

"I have good news," Lukas said. "Maj says you both have good hearts. He will hear your story."

Drake looked up at the Time Dragon. "An evil wizard named Maldred trapped our friend and some wizards inside a wall in his hideout," Drake began.

"And our wizard, Griffith, says they're trapped in time," Rori continued.

"Griffith says that you might have the power to break the spell," Drake said, "because you are a Time Dragon."

After a few seconds, Lukas's Dragon Stone glowed again.

"Maj says he can help," Lukas said. "And he can transport us all to Maldred's hideout in no time."

"My dragon, Worm, can transport, too," Drake told Lukas.

"Is Worm an Earth Dragon?" Lukas asked. "They are very powerful."

"He is," Drake said proudly.

"A Time Dragon's transporting powers are different from an Earth Dragon's," Lukas explained. "Maj can transport to any place, and he can also travel back and forth in time."

Rori was looking up at Maj. "Why is he sitting on a clock?"

"Maj's very first Dragon Master was a clockmaker," Lukas explained. "He built the clock to help train Maj and sharpen his powers. The clock helps Maj transport to more-exact times and places than he can go to on his own."

"Wow, that is a pretty amazing clock," Drake said.

"It is. But it needs a lot of care. I am learning to be a clockmaker myself," Lukas replied. "As Maj's Dragon Master, it is my job to keep the clock running smoothly."

He climbed up some steps on the side of the clock and reached toward the hands.

"Where is Maldred's hideout?" he asked.

"It's inside a magical space," Rori answered.

Lukas moved the hands on the third face of the clock, the one with the strange symbols. He climbed back down the steps.

"Everyone, touch the clock," he instructed.

Drake and Rori reached for the clock. The dragons touched it with their tails.

Lukas looked up at Maj. "We are ready to transport!" he said.

The Time Dragon began to glow with blue light. Drake felt a sizzling energy flow through him. Then he felt an itch on his neck — just like he had felt before leaving Maldred's hideout.

Suddenly, the hands on the clock began to spin wildly.

Lukas frowned. "Who is doing this? The clock hands shouldn't be moving!" he yelled.

The tower filled with Maj's blue light. Then —

Zap! A blast of invisible energy sent Worm, Rori, Vulcan, Lukas, and even Maj flying off the clock.

Drake felt like he was spinning.

Thump! Drake landed in the dirt. He blinked.

He was no longer in the tower. He wasn't in Maldred's hideout, either. He was in an onion field — his family's field. King Roland's castle rose up in the distance.

"Why are we in Bracken?" Drake asked. "Worm, are you okay?"

Drake stood up and looked around. He was all alone.

"Worm?" Drake called out. "Where are you?"

He reached for his Dragon Stone — but it was gone!

WHAT IS HAPPENING?

"Drake, you forgot your basket!" Drake's mother called out as she walked across the field. "And you haven't picked a single onion yet. What have you been doing?"

36

"Mom!" Drake cried. "Something weird has happened! Worm and Rori and Vulcan and I were in the tower of the Time Dragon and we were supposed to transport. But somehow I ended up here all alone! Where is everyone?"

Drake's mother frowned. "Drake, what are you talking about? Who are Worm and Rori and Vulcan? Are you playing some kind of game with your brothers?"

"Mom, you know them," Drake said. "You met them at the castle. Rori is a Dragon Master, just like I am. Worm is my dragon, and Vulcan is hers."

"Drake, dragons aren't real," his mother said.

"But you know they are!" he cried. "You have met Worm yourself." He had a terrible thought: *Did a wizard put a spell on my mom? Did she lose her memory?*

She put her hand on his forehead. "You don't seem to have a fever," she said. "It's fine to make up stories, Drake, but don't get carried away. Finish filling this basket."

"But Mom!" Drake protested.

She walked away.

Drake stared at the onions at his feet. *Something is not right*, he thought. *I've got to get to the castle! Bo, Ana, and Petra will help me!*

Drake ran as fast as he could to King Roland's castle. Along the way, he saw and heard some strange things . . .

The leaves on the trees were starting to turn orange. When he'd left Bracken, it was springtime and the trees were just getting their leaves.

Then, as he passed the marketplace, he heard two women talking.

"King Roland is going to visit Queen Rose in Arkwood," one was saying.

"Wouldn't it be so romantic if they got married?" the other asked.

Drake stopped. "But they *are* married," he told the women. "There was a big wedding parade, with all of the dragons."

"Dragons? Don't be silly, boy. Dragons aren't real," one of the women said, and the two of them walked off, laughing.

Drake was so confused.

"None of this makes sense," he said as he got back on the path to the castle. "I don't have my Dragon Stone. My mom says she's never met Worm. And nobody thinks dragons are real. What is happening?"

"I'll tell you what's happening!" a high, scratchy voice replied.

A tiny creature jumped in front of Drake. She was no taller than Drake's knee. She had big pointy ears and two tiny horns on top of her head. Her body was covered in red fur. Two big eyes stared out of her face.

"Who are you?" Drake asked.

"I am Beezel the Imp!" the creature replied. "And I sent us both back in time!"

THE PAST

Drake's thoughts were spinning.

"What do you mean, you sent us back in time?" he asked the imp.

"Actually, the Time Dragon sent us traveling through time," Beezel replied. "I just changed the clock and used a magical blast to get your friends and dragons off the clock — so only you and I would end up lost in time somewhere."

Beezel held up Drake's Dragon Stone, dangling from its chain. "Oh, and I stole this from you," she added. "So you can't ask your dragon for any help!"

"Give that back!" Drake said, lunging for the imp.

Beezel jumped up onto a tree branch, out of Drake's reach.

"You can't catch me!" she taunted him.

"I don't understand," Drake said. "Why did you do this to me? And how do you know magic?"

"I am an imp, from the Isle of Imps," Beezel replied. "We have magical powers. Not as strong as a wizard's powers, though. Definitely not as strong as Maldred's!"

Drake's eyes got wide. "How do you know Maldred?"

"He took me from my family when I was just a baby imp, and I grew up in his hideout," Beezel replied. "I was happy with Maldred. But then one day he left and never came back. I'm all alone, and now I know it's *your* fault!"

"What do you mean, it's my fault?" Drake asked.

"I heard you and your redheaded friend talking in the hideout today," Beezel said. "You trapped Maldred in a bottle. I'll never see him again."

"Maldred wanted to destroy the world," Drake shot back. "We had to stop him!"

"He was my friend!" the imp cried, stomping her foot. "You made me mad. That's why I turned invisible and hitched a ride on your back and traveled with you to the Time Dragon. Then I messed with the clock so you would be stuck all alone without any friends, just like I am."

Drake gasped. "That's why I felt those itches on my neck!"

Beezel grinned. "Yup! Pretty cool, right? I love turning invisible. Wait, I'll show you."

She squeezed her eyes shut, grunting. Then her eyes fluttered open. "Rats! It's not working! That big blast drained my magic."

Drake gazed around him. "So now we're in the past," he said.

"That's right!" Beezel said with a grin. "I wasn't sure where we would end up, but I like how it turned out. You haven't met your dragon yet. Or any of your friends. You're not Drake the Dragon Master. You're just a regular boy!"

Drake thought quickly. "I can still go to the castle. I'll talk to Worm. He will understand, even if he doesn't recognize me. I can fix this!"

"Ha!" Beezel snorted. "You can't talk to Worm without your Dragon Stone, remember?" She dangled it again.

Drake thought quickly. "I guess you win," he said. He turned his back to her.

"Hee hee!" Beezel cried. "That was easy!"

Drake spun around. He shook the tree branch.

Beezel tumbled off. "Hey!" she yelled.

Drake yanked his Dragon Stone out of her hands. Then he picked up a wooden bucket from a nearby well and dropped it on top of the imp! He topped it with a heavy rock.

"Sorry," he said. "But I need to find Worm and figure out how to get back to my time!"

Drake ran to the castle as fast as he could.

SNEAKING IN

Drake came up with a plan as he ran.

The Training Room guard, Simon, usually naps around this time of day, he remembered, looking up at the sun. *And Griffith and the Dragon Masters should be busy in the classroom. So I will sneak inside Worm's cave and let him know I need his help!*

Drake walked over the stone bridge leading into the castle. Two guards stood at the end of the bridge, watching people enter. Drake spotted a man pulling a cart of potatoes. He ducked behind the cart and followed it inside.

He made his way through the castle halls. He walked past paintings and statues and people in fancy clothes.

Then he reached the stairs. He walked down ... down ... down ... until he came to a big stone door.

The door was cracked open, and Drake peeked in. Simon the guard was leaning against the wall, snoring.

He is napping, just as I thought! Drake tiptoed past him.

Drake heard voices coming from the classroom.

"Dragons can combine their powers," Griffith was saying.

"Ooh!" Ana cried. "Shu and Kepri could combine their powers to make a rainbow!"

"We should try it," Bo agreed.

"This is boring," Rori complained. "Can we go outside now?"

I can't let them see me, he thought. *I just need to talk to Worm.*

Drake held his breath. He tiptoed past the open door. Luckily, his future friends all had their eyes on Griffith.

Then Drake ran into the tunnel that led to the Dragon Caves. Just before he reached the caves, a streak of blue light zoomed past his face.

He looked behind him.

Griffith stood in the tunnel, pointing at Drake. Blue sparks of magic flashed on the end of his finger.

"Stop right there!" he commanded.

CHAPTER 10

FIND THE TRUTH

riffith, let me explain!" Drake said. "My name is Drake. I am a Dragon Master. And I am here because of Maldred's imp!"

The wizard's eyes narrowed, but he did not lower his finger. "How do you know of Maldred? What kingdom are you from? And who is your dragon?"

55

"Worm — Oh, my dragon doesn't have a name yet, but he's an Earth Dragon," Drake began. "You see —"

Griffith took a step closer to Drake. "That dragon doesn't have a Dragon Master." He pointed to the Dragon Stone around Drake's neck. "Did you steal that?"

"No! I didn't steal anything," Drake replied. "I am not Worm's Dragon Master *yet*. But I *will* be in the future."

"How can you be from the future?" Griffith asked.

"We went to see the Time Dragon in the Land of Casgore for help with a mission," Drake explained.

"Maldred's imp messed with the clock and we were sent back in time — to this time."

Griffith lowered his finger.

"Interesting," he said. "You may be telling the truth, but how can I be sure? You could have been sent here by Maldred to trick me."

"I would *never* help Maldred," Drake said.

Griffith frowned. "Then why did you sneak into the castle?"

"I wasn't sure you would believe me," Drake said. "But I think my dragon might, so I was trying to get to him."

"There is only one way to find out if you are telling the truth," Griffith said. "Let's go to the Dragon Caves!"

WILL WE CONNECT?

Drake and Griffith walked farther into the tunnel.

Drake looked down at his Dragon Stone. *Will Worm and I be able to connect?* he wondered.

When they reached the end of the tunnel, Drake ran to Worm's cave. The dragon was curled up, sleeping.

"Hi there! I know you don't know me yet. But it's me, Drake!" Drake said. "I am your Dragon Master."

The dragon lifted his head. He stared at Drake with his big green eyes.

"I'm from the future. That's why you don't know me. You see, today I was sent back in time," Drake explained. "But in the future we'll go on a lot of missions together, and I know about your special powers."

Griffith frowned. "I do not know if this will work, Drake. Even if this dragon *does* have great powers," he said, "I don't think you can expect to have a strong enough connection to —"

Suddenly, Drake's Dragon Stone began to glow bright green. He heard Worm's voice clearly inside his head.

I feel like I know you, Worm said.

Drake answered him. *That's because we are good friends.*

I can feel our connection, Worm said. *I believe you.*

Drake turned to Griffith, who was staring at the Dragon Stone with wide eyes.

"I see your Dragon Stone glowing," the wizard said. "I believe you now."

Drake smiled. "Thanks! I am just not sure what to do next. I know that my dragon and I can transport anywhere in the world together. But he can't travel through time."

"I may have a solution," Griffith said. "Ask your dragon to transport you to Casgore. Then you can ask the Time Dragon to send you back to your time."

Drake nodded. "That might work," he said. "Hopefully, I'll see you in the future, Griffith. Wish me luck."

"Good luck," the wizard said.

Drake reached into Worm's cave and touched his neck.

"Please transport us to the home of the Time Dragon in the Land of Casgore," Drake said.

Worm's body began to glow. But just as they were about to transport, Drake heard a voice behind him. "Not so fast! Wait for me!"

Beezel zoomed into the Dragon Caves. The imp jumped on top of Griffith's head, knocking off his hat. "Beezel weasel will always win it!" she cried. "Empty your head this very minute!"

Griffith blinked.
"No!" Drake yelled.

Beezel jumped on Drake's back as the cave filled with Worm's green light, and they transported in a flash.

UPSIDE DOWN

"Get off of me!" Drake cried when they appeared in Casgore. They were in front of the white house and the stone tower.

65

Beezel jumped off his back. "Thanks for the ride!"

"What did you do to Griffith before we left?" Drake asked. "Is he okay?"

"I just wiped his memory of the last five minutes," she said. "I don't want him coming to help you again."

Drake shook his head. "Why do you have to be so mean?" he asked.

"You know why!" Beezel replied. "Anyway, you were pretty clever, sticking me under that bucket. But it didn't take long for my powers to come back so I could escape."

Beezel looked around. "Now I guess you came here so you could get back to your time. Not if I can help it!" she cried. She spun around. "Flip, flop, feet on top!"

Drake's body lurched up into the air, then turned upside down!

"Stop that!" Drake yelled.

Beezel grinned. "No way! This is fun!"

"Beezel, put me down!" Drake said. "Or I'll tell Worm to . . ."

"To what? To blast me?" Beezel asked. "You'd still be stuck in this spell."

"Please, Beezel," Drake pleaded. "I just want to get home to my friends."

Beezel crossed her arms. "Why should I help you do that when I have lost my only friend, thanks to you?"

"You can live with me and my friends," Drake said.

Beezel shook her head. "No way! Not after what you all did to Maldred."

I can't imagine missing Maldred! Drake thought, but then he remembered that the workshop was the only home the imp had ever known. Except . . .

Drake looked over at Worm. He had a thought.

"What if Worm transported you to the Isle of Imps?" Drake asked Beezel. "There would be other imps there. You could find your family."

"Hmm," Beezel said. "That is not a bad idea."

"So will you put me down?" Drake asked.

She nodded. "It's a deal!"

Drake grinned.

Then Beezel chanted again. "Feet back down, on the ground!"

Drake's body flipped in the air and he softly landed on the grass.

"Now let's find Lukas and Maj and get me back to the future," said Drake. He rushed into the stone tower, followed by Worm and Beezel.

BACK TO THE FUTURE

Drake looked around. Lukas was not in the tower, but Maj was perched on his clock, just like before. Drake asked Worm to explain his story to the Time Dragon.

Maj's body began to glow. Blue beams shot out of his eyes and hit Drake, just like they had when Drake first saw Maj. Drake's body tingled.

A moment later, Drake's Dragon Stone glowed. He heard Worm's voice in his head. *Maj said no explanation is necessary. Maj knows you from the future. He will send you back there.*

"Great!" Drake said.

But there is something you must do first, Worm said. *Lukas is away. So Maj says you must move the hands of the clock.* He sent a picture to Drake's mind of how the clock should look.

Drake climbed the steps, like Lukas had done before, and moved the hands on the first and second faces of the clock.

"Like this?" Drake asked, and Maj nodded. Drake climbed down and looked at Worm.

"When you leave," he told his dragon, "please take Beezel to the Isle of Imps. And then transport yourself back to Bracken Castle."

Worm nodded. *I will.*

Drake patted his neck. "Thanks for your help. I'll catch up with you in the future."

I am looking forward to it, Worm said. *I was not happy in King Roland's castle. But now that I know I have a good Dragon Master, I will no longer worry.*

Drake hugged him. "Thanks again."

Beezel jumped on Worm's neck. "Take me to the Isle of Imps!"

"I'm supposed to say that," Drake said. "But yes, please transport."

Worm's body glowed green.

Beezel waved. "Goood-byeeeeeeeee!" she called out.

Then Worm and Beezel vanished in a flash of green light.

The Time Dragon began to glow and the tower filled with bright blue light. A sizzling energy flowed through Drake and he closed his eyes. Drake felt the tower spin.

When he opened his eyes, he was still in the tower — but he was back in the future! Lukas and Rori were sprawled on the floor. Maj was climbing back on top of the clock. Vulcan was getting back on his feet. Worm floated over to Drake, and Drake patted his tail.

"I am sorry," Lukas said. "Something went wrong. Is everyone okay?"

"I'm fine," Rori reported. "What happened?"

"I will explain everything later," Drake said. "Right now, we need Maj to take us to Maldred's hideout so we can free Eko from the wall."

"Yes!" Rori agreed.

They all touched the clock again. Maj glowed with blue light.

Then the tower began to spin . . .

BREAKING THE SPELL

The three Dragon Masters and their dragons appeared in the top of Maldred's hideout.

"You made it!" Griffith said. "Good work, Rori and Drake!"

He knows me, Drake thought. *I am so thankful to be back in my own time!*

"There was a little problem, but we made it," Drake replied.

Griffith turned to Lukas. "You must be the Time Dragon's Dragon Master."

"Yes, I am Lukas," the boy replied. He smiled at Griffith. "What do you get if you cross a wizard with a blizzard?"

Before anyone could answer, Lukas said, "A cold spell. Get it?"

Griffith laughed. "Clever!"

Lukas ran his fingers across the faces.

"Wow," he said. "I can feel the wall tingling. Like they're alive in there."

"They *are* alive. They're just trapped in time," Rori said. "Now can you and Maj please rescue Eko?" She glanced over at Neru. He was still staring sadly at Eko's face.

"When Maj breaks the spell, he will free *everyone* trapped inside the wall," Lukas said. "Not just Eko."

"I thought so," Griffith said. He held up a book. "I found Maldred's journal. He lists all of the wizards he has trapped in the wall. I haven't finished reading the list, but Maldred's enemies were both good *and* bad. Some evil wizards could go free."

"We have to take that chance to save Eko," Rori said.

"Rori's right," Drake agreed.

"Then let's proceed," Griffith said.

Lukas looked at his dragon. "Maj, please break this time spell!" he commanded.

Maj's body glowed. Blue light swirled from his eyes. It hit the wall and then began to ripple around the top of the tower. It lit up all the faces.

The light grew brighter and brighter. Wizards, their whole bodies glowing blue, stepped out of the wall.

The light began to fade. Wizards filled the hall. Tall wizards and short wizards. Wizards with beards and wizards with curly hair. Old wizards and young wizards.

Griffith ran to a gray-haired wizard in black robes. "Ezzie! Good to see you, old friend!" He gave her a hug.

Drake spotted a wizard with long, red hair. Her furry robes looked familiar. Then she snapped her fingers.

Poof! She disappeared.

Poof! Poof! Poof! Poof! More wizards used magic to disappear.

Then one tall black-haired woman, not wearing wizard's robes, stepped out of the wall.

"Eko!" Rori cried.

ON THE LOOSE!

Eko hugged Neru. The dragon nuzzled her with his furry snout.

"How did you find me?" she asked.

Her Dragon Stone glowed green as Neru answered.

Eko turned to Rori. "Thank you for saving me," she said, hugging her.

"We had to," Rori said. "You saved me and Drake from Maldred."

"I am sorry I ever agreed to help Maldred," Eko said. "I thought he wanted dragons to be free, like I do. I didn't think he would ever try to destroy the world — or hurt you two."

"It's okay," Rori told her.

The rescued wizards, the ones who hadn't poofed away, were looking around, dazed.

"Where am I?" asked a wizard with frizzy purple hair.

"You will not get me, Maldred!" cried a wizard wearing brown robes. He swirled around, waving his wand.

Griffith's voice boomed over the crowd. "Calm down, everyone! Maldred trapped you in time. But you are not in danger anymore. Maldred is not here, and you are free. We can help you get home."

The wizards all began to talk at once.

"Follow me," Griffith said. "We'll sort this out." He led them downstairs.

"Was it scary inside the wall?" Rori asked Eko.

"Not really," Eko said. "I knew I was trapped. But it only felt like seconds. How long has it been? And where is Maldred?"

"It's a long story," Rori said.

Lukas interrupted them. "And now you have plenty of *time* to tell it," he said.

"This is Lukas and his Time Dragon, Maj," Drake told Eko. "They're the ones who really broke the spell."

"Thank you both," Eko said.

"You're welcome," Lukas said. He turned to Drake and Rori. "Maj and I must return home. But you should visit us when you can."

"Sure," Drake said. "I'm sure we'll have a good *time*."

Lukas grinned. Then Maj's body glowed and they transported back to Casgore.

Drake, Rori, and Eko brought their dragons downstairs to Maldred's workshop. They found Griffith leafing through Maldred's journal. A few wizards were standing around the desk, drinking tea.

"These are the wizards who, like me, can't magically transport," Griffith explained. "Worm can help us get them home. But we have another problem."

"What's that?" Drake asked.

Griffith tapped the book with his finger. "There are definitely evil wizards on this list. Some of them are even worse than Maldred."

Drake gasped. "And now they're on the loose!"

"Yes, I'm afraid so," Griffith replied.

"What do you think they'll do?" Drake wondered.

Griffith shook his head. "I don't know. But we must be ready to stop them."

"I will help you," Eko said.

Griffith smiled. "It is good to have you back, Eko," he said.

Rori smiled at her, too. "Evil wizards don't stand a chance against the Dragon Masters!" she said.

Drake nodded. "We'll be ready for them!"

TRACEY WEST loves reading tales of dragons from around the world. Maj the Time Dragon gets his look from a dragon that is the symbol of the country of Slovenia. One bridge there is decorated with twenty dragon statues! Tracey has written dozens of books for kids. She lives in New York's Catskill Mountains with her husband, pets, and a flock of chickens.

DANIEL GRIFFO lives in Argentina with his wife, Elba, and their two children, Valentina and Benjamin. As a child, Daniel loved creating and drawing pictures. He worked hard to develop his artistic skills. At the age of seventeen, he got his first illustration job and then he gained experience working for several large companies. Daniel looks at each project as a new adventure. He always enjoys exploring the wonderful world of illustration.

DRAGON MASTERS
FUTURE OF THE TIME DRAGON

Questions and Activities

Worm and Maj can both transport, but their powers work differently. How do Worm's powers work? How do Maj's work?

Beezel sends Drake to the past. Why does she do this?

When Beezel puts a spell on Drake, she says "Flip, flop, feet on top!" *Flop* and *top* rhyme. Make a list of other words that rhyme with *flop* and *top*.

Lukas likes to tell jokes. One of his jokes is that a wizard and a blizzard make a "cold spell." Why is this funny?

When Drake returns to the future, he tells Rori that he will explain everything later. Pretend YOU are Drake. Write a letter to Rori explaining why you went to Bracken. Draw pictures of what you saw and who you talked to!